THE GODDI OF THE KITCHEN

AND OTHER STORIES

Folktales from Africa

Kolapo Oyefeso

Spectrum Books Limited
Ibadan
Abuja • Benin City • Lagos • Owerri

Spectrum titles can be purchased on line at
www.spectrumbooksonline.com

Published by
Spectrum Books Limited
Spectrum House
Ring Road
P. M. B. 5612
Ibadan, Nigeria

in association with
Safari Books (Export) Limited
1st Floor
17 Bond Street
St. Helier
Jersey JE2 3NP
Channel Islands
United Kingdom

Europe and USA Distributor
African Books Collective Ltd.,
The Jam Factory,
27 Park End Street,
Oxford OX1, 1HU, UK.

First published 2000
Reprinted 2001

ISBN: 978-029-176-8

Printed by Meg-Comm Network

CONTENTS

Rosalie-Ann

1

The Sky and the Earth

A long time ago there were seven earths and seven skies. The Great God created the seven earths and seven skies and each earth and each sky had its own lesser god.

Everything went well until one day the earth quarrelled with the sky. The earth had declared that it was older than the sky; that was what started the quarrel. The Great God, who lived between the seventh earth and the seventh sky, heard about the quarrel and was annoyed. The Great God then knocked down the iron post that held the sky above the earth and the sky fell on to the earth. All the lesser gods of the other worlds did the same (they always copied whatever the Great God did) and the skies came falling down on to the earths.

All the animals and people and plants on the seven earths were crushed. All, except the elders who, when they saw the sky falling, knew it was not a good thing and changed into snakes. The earth, seeing what the sky had done, agreed that the sky was stronger and...yes, older. The Great God was pleased and He put the iron post up again – but not as high as before. The Great God wanted the earth to see the sky close by and remember. All the other gods followed their leader. The Great God then created human beings again but because the sky was so low the people could not grow.

The sky disturbed the women when they raised the pestles of their mortars and, one day, an old woman took her pestle and pushed the sky far away. People were now able to grow, and till this day the sky is where she pushed it.

2

Why the Sky is far above the Earth

A long time ago, God created heaven and earth. God looked at the earth and liked it. God now created people and animals to make it even better, and told them that everything they could see was theirs to use. The earth was fresh and green with rich forests, clean air and excellent weather. God placed the sky close to the earth, low enough for people to reach up and touch it. The sky, God said, was food for them to share, and the earth was theirs to enjoy. Whenever people felt hungry, all they had to do was reach up and cut a piece of the sky.

God then warned them that no one was to cut more of the sky than he or she could eat at a time. If they did, God said, they would all be punished. The sky would no longer be food for them because God would raise it and no one would be able to reach it.

For a long time everyone was content with God's plan. The earth was a good place and the people and the animals were happy. Then one day a man called Aseju, who thought he was smarter than most people, told a friend of his that even though the sky was vast, he was certain the time would come when it would all be gone. His friend thought a bit about this and then asked him if he was sure.

'Yes,' Aseju answered, 'I am. And where do you think we will all be if that happens?'

'Ah,' said his friend whose name was Dundu, 'umm ... where?'

'Out looking for food, that's where,' Aseju snapped at him. 'No more easy pickings.'

The picture became clearer to Dundu. He nodded. He asked Aseju what they were going to do about it. Aseju whispered into his ear that they were going to cut more than they could eat and hide it away.

'Bu-but what if people find out?' Dundu asked.

'They won't find out if someone we know doesn't tell them,' Aseju smiled.

'Hahaha,' Dundu laughed, 'umm ... who?'

'You, foolish man. If you do not tell anyone, not even God will know!'

So Aseju and Dundu cut large portions of the sky, ate some and hid the rest. In their greed they cut more and more, doing what is today called 'cornering the market.' The secret leaked, as it always does, and other people joined in the scramble for the sky.

The sky became smaller and smaller. God was furious. Sending down bolts of lightning and thundering in anger, God moved the sky high above the earth. From that time on, men and women have had to toil for their food and the earth is no longer the peaceful and beautiful place it used to be.

3

Tortoise Loses his Oranges

Early one morning, Tortoise put on his battered straw hat and set out for Oje market. He had found some oranges growing wild and was now taking them to the market to sell. This market was far from his home – which is why Tortoise set out so early – and he had to travel through a thick forest, climb a hill or two and cross a river. He had almost reached the market when he suddenly felt very thirsty. He knew there was a well nearby so he left his basket of oranges by the roadside and went to get some cool water.

While Tortoise was drinking, Monkey came skipping along the road and saw the oranges. Monkey was not really hungry but since oranges were there and no one was watching over them, he decided to help himself. The oranges were delicious and Monkey was eating the last one when Tortoise came back.

'Wha-what are you doing? Those are my oranges!' Tortoise shouted.

Monkey was startled at first. He put the last half-eaten orange down slowly and said, 'I found some oranges by the roadside and so they became mine.'

'Why, you silly animal, how do you think they got there?' Tortoise retorted.

'It is not a habit of mine to question oranges,' Monkey answered haughtily, 'and now, if you do not mind, I shall be on my way.'

It was Monkey's plan to get away before Tortoise accused him of being a thief but Tortoise was not having any of that.

Rosalie-Ann

'Oh no, you shall not!' he shouted, grabbing Monkey by the waist. 'You are going to pay me for those oranges.'

'I found them! They are mine!' Monkey screeched. He tried to free his arm but Tortoise held on fast. 'Let go of my arm!' Monkey struggled. 'The oranges belong to me.'

'No, they don't, you thief!' Tortoise said. 'They are mine and you must pay me for them!'

Tortoise and Monkey argued and struggled. Monkey refused to pay for the oranges and Tortoise would not let him go. So, to settle the matter, they went to the king.

The king listened to them. After hearing first one argument and then the other he ruled that the oranges belonged to Monkey.

'It is our custom,' he declared, 'If anyone finds a thing on the road, it belongs to him.'

Tortoise shuffled home sad but wiser.

A few weeks later, Tortoise was walking through the forest when he saw Monkey fast asleep by the path. Monkey's head was on a rock and his tail was across the road. Tortoise stared at Monkey's tail and smiled a wicked smile. He got hold of the tail and pulled it hard. Monkey woke up and tried to free himself but Tortoise would not let go. They argued and struggled and, to settle the matter, they went to the king.

Again the king listened to them and ruled, 'The tail belongs to Tortoise. He found it on the road.'

So Monkey's tail was cut off and given to Tortoise.

Tortoise went home happily. Monkey was sorry he had taken the oranges, and from that day on he never took anything without asking.

4

The Hand that Helps

In the highlands, there is a wide river that flows from the hills, through the savannah grasslands and all the way to the sea. During the rains, the river floods the plains and when the water falls, the land is left fertile and well watered. The farmers start to plant their crops in the rich soil as soon as the water level drops.

One season, the river spread further than usual and the farmers were happy. They waited eagerly for the water to ebb so they could plant their millet, sorghum and maize. One of the farmers, a man called Ali, left home daily to check the water level. He was an impatient sort of man.

One morning, Ali set out on his donkey and found that the flood had receded. He hurried back to the village with the good news. As he was riding back, stopping now and then to inspect the soil, he saw a huge crocodile. The crocodile had been left far behind when the water receded suddenly, and now he was dying. Ali went over to the crocodile.

'What will you give me if I help you to the river?' Ali asked.

The crocodile opened one eye, looked at Ali and said slowly, 'I promise that none of the crocodiles in the river will ever attack anyone from your village again.'

Ali thought this was a good thing so he got down, placed the crocodile on the donkey and tied him so that he would stay on. He led the donkey to the riverbank and there he untied the crocodile

Rosalie-Ann

and helped him down. As Ali turned to go, the crocodile opened its mouth and seized Ali's arm. 'Now I am going to eat you,' said the crocodile, 'for I am very hungry.'

Ali protested loudly but the crocodile would not let him go. At that moment a hyena was passing by and asked what was happening. Ali spoke first and then the crocodile, but the hyena pretended not to understand their stories.

'Did you say your donkey carried the crocodile here? How? You tied him? How was he tied? I don't understand! Show me. What did you tie him with? This same rope here? You tied it round his legs? Like that? And across his body, his front legs as well?' The hyena went on like this until Ali had tied up the crocodile again to show him how it had been done.

'Now leave him,' the sly hyena said. 'For helping you, I think I'll have his innards and you can have the rest.'

Ali took out his knife and shared the crocodile with the hyena.

Never bite the hand that helps you and never trust a crocodile ... or a hyena.

5

The Hunter and the Bow

There was once a hunter who owned the best bow anyone had ever seen. It was an excellent bow – strong, light and supple. When he shot an arrow with it, the arrow flew faster, further and hit its target more often than those of the other hunters. The other hunters would stand and watch, their eyes shining with envy.

One day, the hunter was rubbing oil into his bow to keep it strong and supple when an idea occurred to him.

'If I make this bow a little bit thinner,' he thought, 'it will even be better. It will be more supple and my arrows will fly faster and truer.'

With him, to think was to do and so he brought out his knife and whittled the bow down.

He tried the bow and he thought it was better, but only just so. So he decided to whittle some more. He tried the bow again and as he pulled the string the bow suddenly snapped, much to his surprise and dismay. The hunter had lost his most valuable possession.

Trying to make a good thing better sometimes destroys it.

6

The Elephant and the Monkey

The Elephant looked at the Monkey and said, 'You must obey me. Whatever I tell you to do, you must do.'

The monkey did not like this at all. 'Why must I obey you?' he asked.

'Because I am bigger, stronger and more important than you,' the elephant answered.

'Look at you! You are ... you are almost nothing.'

The monkey did not know what to say. The elephant walked away feeling happy that he had oppressed the monkey. He raised his trunk and blew loudly, trumpeting for the forest to hear.

Some hunters who had been having a hard time finding any prey heard him and came looking. They saw the elephant, took aim and fired. The elephant fell with a loud crash and the monkey scampered up a tree and escaped.

He was almost nothing, so the hunters took no notice of him.

7

The Nightingale and the Pig

One evening the nightingale sang a beautiful song. Several animals passed beneath the tree where she was perched and they stopped to praise her song. They told her the song was the best they had ever heard and the nightingale was thrilled. Their admiration made her sing even better.

The pig was passing. He had eaten a lot at lunch and was taking a walk so he could work up an appetite for dinner. He heard the nightingale and stopped to listen. When the nightingale finished, the pig grunted, 'Very nice, my feathered friend, but in our compound we have a cock who sings every morning and he can sing much louder than you can. Much, much louder. You can't beat that!'

The nightingale was upset. She was disturbed. She shed a little tear and could not sing again. An owl who had been enjoying her song, nodding and tapping his feet to the beat, heard what the pig said and spoke to the nightingale.

'Dear nightingale,' he said, 'never waste your talent on someone with no taste.'

Rosalie-Ann

8

Tortoise, Elephant and Hippopotamus

Tortoise was broke. He sat in front of his house with his head down, looking worried. How can I make some money without having to work? he wondered. Tortoise hated working. He got up and went for a walk hoping to find an answer to his problem.

As he was slowly climbing a hill in the forest, he met Elephant who trumpeted, 'Out of my way, lazybones, I have work to do.'

Tortoise stopped, looked up at Elephant towering above him, and had an idea.

'Ah, Elephant,' he said, 'you do make a lot of noise, don't you? I am sure I can work as hard, or even harder than you can.

'Hehehe! Haha!' Elephant laughed. 'You! Haha! You tell a good joke but you can't work.'

'But I can,' said Tortoise. 'I am as strong as you are and I can do as much work.'

'As strong as I am?' Elephant was annoyed. 'Don't be ridiculous,' he snapped.

'Do you want to bet?' asked tricky Tortoise.

Elephant nodded and Tortoise hurried to the river, which was on the other side of the hill. There he met Hippopotamus going back to the river after feeding all night.

'Mr. Hippo!' he called. All Hippopotamus's friends called him Hippo because his name was a bit of a mouthful. Hippo stopped and Tortoise said, 'I have been watching you and I bet that I am as strong as you are.'

Now, Hippo was an animal who never said much. He looked at Tortoise, yawned loudly and said, 'Don't be an idiot.'

Tortoise told him that he was serious and he could prove it. 'I'll bet you ten thousand cowries that if we have a tug-of-war, you won't be able to pull me.'

Hippo agreed and Tortoise brought out a long rope. He told Hippo to hold it between his teeth and pull only when he, Tortoise, shouted, "Go!"

Tortoise then ran up the hill and down the other side where he found Elephant waiting for him.

'Thought you got scared and decided not to come,' Elephant rumbled.

'I am here,' answered Tortoise, 'and I am ready. All you have to do is hold on to this rope and pull when you hear me shout "Go!"'

Tortoise hurried up the hill to a place where he could see Elephant and Hippo and they could not see him. 'Go!' he shouted, and both Elephant and Hippopotamus pulled.

They both thought Tortoise was at the other end of the rope. They pulled and tugged and pulled. Neither one could pull the other. After a while they got tired of pulling and agreed that Tortoise was far stronger than they had imagined. Tortoise won the bet and he quickly collected his money while they were still too tired to ask questions.

Some days later Elephant met Hippo and while talking they realised that Tortoise had tricked both of them. They were too ashamed to tell anyone but they agreed never to wager with someone they could not trust.

9

The Hare and the Baboon

The hare and the baboon spent many hours together, playing and hunting for food. They were good friends. One day the baboon, who thought himself clever, decided to play a trick on the hare. He brewed some beer and invited the hare for a drink. When the hare arrived, the baboon took the calabash of beer and climbed up a tree.

'Come on up,' he said, sipping at the beer and smacking his lips, 'the beer's very nice.' The baboon knew the hare could not climb and it amused him to see the hare watching him drink the beer.

'You know I can't climb,' the hare pleaded. 'Why don't you come down?'

'Hahaha! Sorry,' the baboon laughed. 'If you want some, you've got to climb.' The hare was angry. He watched the baboon drinking the beer and got angrier and angrier. After a while he went off in a temper without tasting any of the beer. When he got home he decided that he was going to play a trick of his own on the baboon.

A few days later the hare sent out invitations for a party. He told everyone that there would be plenty to eat and drink at his party and they must all come. He sent a special invitation to the baboon. On the day of the party, the hare burnt all the tall grass around his house. Then he cooked the food and got the drinks. When he finished, he sat down and waited for his guests to arrive.

The baboon was the first to arrive. The hare welcomed him and asked him to eat.

RosalieAnn

'But, before you start,' he said, you must let me see your hands.'

The baboon was surprised but he showed his hands. They were dirty from the ash outside the hare's house.

'What dirty hands you have!' the hare exclaimed. 'You can't eat with such dirty hands. You must go and wash them.'

The baboon went off to wash his hands. On the way back he had to walk over the freshly burnt grass and his hands became dirty again. The hare told him that he could not eat unless his hands were clean. Back and forth the baboon went. All the other animals had arrived and while they were eating, the baboon was washing his hands and getting them dirty again.

At last, all the delicious food was eaten and the refreshing drinks drunk. The baboon went home hot, bothered and angry, without eating a single bite.

10

The King and the Thinker

There was once a king who had a problem. His problem was that the farmers in his kingdom did not know how to store the grains they harvested. After every harvest, all the rice, sorghum, maize and millet that were not used within a few weeks had to be thrown away. The king called all the wise men and women in the kingdom to find a solution. They thought and thought but none of their suggestions worked very well.

One day a courtier ran up to the king and told him there was a stranger in the marketplace saying he could solve the problem. The king sent for the stranger and when he arrived, asked him if he knew how to store grain so it would last from one season to the next. The man, whose name was Ironu, said 'Yes, Kabiyesi, I do.'

'Well,' said the king, 'that is wonderful! If you can show our farmers how to do it, and if it works, I shall give you anything you ask for.'

'Thank you, Kabiyesi,' Ironu said.

'Do not thank me yet,' the king warned him, 'for if you fail, you are a dead man.'

The threat made Ironu pause for thought, and then he assured the king that it would work. 'I have tried and tested the method,' he said. 'It works.'

The king gave Ironu everything he asked for and in sixty days Ironu had built several silos for the grains and shown the farmers how to keep pests away. The kingdom now held its breath and waited to see if the grains would keep till the next season. While

RosalieAnn

they waited, the king invited Ironu to live in the palace with him. They became friends and often sat and talked till late at night.

'How come you know so much?' Kabiyesi asked.

'I have travelled a lot and seen many things,' answered Ironu. 'I also read a lot and think about everything I see or read.

'You shouldn't think so much,' said Kabiyesi. 'Being too clever is not good for one's health. It leaves you no time to have fun.'

After several months had passed, the grain silos were opened and inspected. All the different grains had kept well and the king was delighted. He called his courtiers to the palace and told them that the time had come to reward Ironu. He reminded them of his promise to Ironu and asked him to name his reward.

Ironu thought for a while and then said, 'Kabiyesi, I worked on the silos for sixty days. I would like you to give me one cowry for the first day and then twice that for the next day, doubling it everyday for the sixty days I worked.'

'Can you say that again?' asked the king. He was not very good with figures.

'For the first day I worked, Kabiyesi will give me one cowry,' Ironu explained, and for the next day, two cowries. For the third day I shall receive four cowries and for the fourth day, eight ... and so on for sixty days. For each day, Kabiyesi will give me twice what he gave me for the day before.'

'Ah,' said Kabiyesi, nodding, 'that should not be a problem.' He turned to the keeper of the treasury and told him to bring out the cowries.

It wasn't until they got the payment for the fourteenth day, that the king felt there might be a small problem. When they counted out the cowries for the twentieth day – over a million of them– 1,048,576 to be precise – and they still had to double this forty times, the king realised that he had a major problem. He stopped the counting.

'You will remember, my dear Ironu,' he said sadly, 'that I told you too much thinking and being too clever can be dangerous to one's health.'

He then called for his executioner and had Ironu beheaded.

11

The Goddess of the Kitchen

In a town at the edge of a desert there lived two sisters. One of them was called Alia and she was very rich. She lived in a big house with marble walls and fountains and had many servants. Her children were always well fed and well clothed. Alia also had a large stall in the bazaar where she bought things cheap and sold them dearly. This was how she became rich. All the other traders thought her very clever.

Her sister, Nadia, was very poor. She and her children often went hungry. They never had any money and Nadia did not want to beg.

One day, when they had not eaten for two days – all they had was water – she swallowed her pride and went to her sister's house to ask for food. After she had been kept waiting for a long time, she saw Alia who refused to give her any food.

'I work hard for the food we eat,' she said, 'I can't give it away.'

Nadia went down on her knees and begged. She cried in shame and then begged some more. Alia felt guilty and said the best she could do was give her the food she kept for her goats – the leftover food. Now her goats would have to go hungry, she complained, and they would not grow, and she would not make as much money on them.

The goddess of the kitchen, who was passing by, heard all that Nadia and Alia said and she cast spell on Alia's kitchen. The next time Alia and her children sat to eat, the rice was mixed with maggots, the bread was green and smelled like a dirty, damp

Rosalie·Ann

cloth and the meat tasted like leather. The food could not be eaten. Alia was horrified and her children wept from hunger. All the food in the house was strange; it was all right until they sat down to eat, then it would change and become awful.

Alia was worried and upset. She went to see the old soothsayer. He gazed into a bowl of clear water and saw what had happened.

'You have done wrong, my daughter,' he said, 'and the goddess of the kitchen is angry.'

'But what have I done?'

The soothsayer gazed into the bowl again. 'You did not give food to someone in need and the goddess put a spell on your kitchen. The only food you will be able to eat will be food that you share.'

Alia remembered Nadia and was ashamed.

'What should I do?' she asked.

The soothsayer told her that she had to share her food with others whenever she wished to eat. 'But that is not a problem,' he added. 'Don't you know that the best food is food that you share?'

12

The Clever Carpenter

There was once a king who had only one daughter. Her name was Enitan and she was so beautiful that stories were told and songs sung about her. Young men came from far and near to marry her. Princes and merchants, teachers and soldiers, they all came to ask for her hand but Enitan did not want any of them. She wanted to marry someone she would love.

The king was worried. He wanted his daughter to marry someone she would be happy with, but he felt that she was being too choosy.

'Enitan,' he asked one day, 'don't you like any of the princes?'

'They are all nice, Papa,' she answered.

'But isn't there one that you really like?'

'No, Papa.'

The king then asked her what kind of man she wanted and she said someone who was handsome and kind and who would make her laugh. He nodded and said he would think about it.

A week later he called Enitan and told her that he had a plan.

'You want someone who can make you laugh, don't you?' he asked.

'Er, yes, Papa,' answered Enitan, wondering what her father had in mind.

'Good, good,' he smiled. 'You will marry the first man who can tell a good story for one week. That way we will be sure that he can make you laugh and keep you laughing.' The king felt it was a good plan. 'And anyone,' he said as another thought came to him, 'anyone who tries and fails shall pay me a thousand cowries.' This made the plan exceptional as far as he was concerned.

The king sent for the town crier at once. When the princes and merchants, the teachers and soldiers heard the news, they were all delighted. They were sure that one of them would win Enitan's hand. They went to the palace to tell their stories but one by one they all failed. Some stories were funny, some were strange but none went on for more than a day. They all had to pay the king, who consoled them and took their money.

When the last of the rich and important men had failed, a man got up from the crowd of people listening and bowed to the king. 'Kabiyesi, he said, 'I would like to try.'

Everyone looked at him and a ripple of comments ran through the crowd. 'It's Tanmo,' someone said. 'Is he all right?' another asked. 'He must have a fever, because he certainly doesn't have any money to pay the king if he fails,' someone else said.

'Who are you?' the king asked.

'I am Tanmo the carpenter,' he answered

'Do you know what will happen if you fail?'

'I do.'

'Very well,' said the king, 'you may begin.'

Tanmo was afraid. He knew a good story but he was not sure how to make it last. He tried to speak but he could not. His mouth was dry. He swallowed and stuttered a few times and the king gave him a stern look.

Tanmo looked up and saw Enitan staring at him. She smiled and suddenly he felt much better. He started his story.

'It was a good harvest. The farmers were happy. They had worked hard and now all the crops were gathered. On the last day of the harvest, one of the farmers noticed a dark cloud in the sky and he thought it was about to rain. As he watched, the cloud came lower and lower and the farmer realised that it was not rain.

' "Locusts!" he shouted, and almost immediately the swarm

Rosalie-Ann

descended on the crops.

'There were locusts everywhere; thousands and thousands of insects fell on the gathered crops and covered the field like a carpet. The farmers had to flee. They stood at a distance and watched the locusts eating all their crops.'

The crowd listening to Tanmo sighed in sympathy. Tanmo went on. 'It was a sad time for the villagers. They thought that perhaps they had done something wrong. They prayed and made offering to appease their gods. The farmers met to decide what to do if the locusts came again and one of them had an idea. He told the others that if they built a store, it would keep locusts and other pests away from their crops. They thought it was a good idea and they all worked hard to build one.

The next year all the crops were kept in the store and on the last day of the harvest the locusts came again. They swarmed around the store but they could not get at the crops. They went round and round, buzzing angrily until a locust found a small hole in the wall. It went in, took a grain and crept out. Another locust went in, took a grain and crept out. Then another locust went in, took a grain and crept out. And yet another locust went in ...'

Tanmo went on like this for a while – each locust going in, taking a grain and creeping out – until the king shouted: 'Hold it! We have heard all that. What happened next?'

"But, Kabiyesi, the story has just started. I must tell you how the locusts emptied the granary. The hole was big enough for only one locust at a time and I have told you how thirty-seven locusts went in and came out."

Enitan laughed. Her father frowned. 'Go on,' he said to Tanmo.

'Thank you, Kabiyesi. Then another locust went in, took a grain and crept out. Then another locust went in, took a grain and crept out. And another locust went in ...'

The king fell asleep. When he woke up Tanmo was still telling the story.

'How many locusts have gone in now?' asked the king.

'Seven hundred and nine, Kabiyesi,' Tanmo answered.

'I see,' said the king wearily. 'Well, the other locusts can wait till tomorrow.'

'Yes, Kabiyesi.'

The king stood up and the royal party departed. Tanmo had told his story for one day. He had six more days to go.

The next day Tanmo continued his story.

'Another locust went in, took a grain and crept out. Another followed, took a grain and crept out. Then another went in, took a grain and crept out. Another one ...'

The king was annoyed. 'Listen, young man,' he said. 'This is becoming too much.'

'But, Kabiyesi,' Tanmo replied, 'the locusts mean to empty the store. There is only way in and they can go in only one at a time.'

'Can't they find another way in?'

'They are locusts, Kabiyesi. They are not very clever.'

Tanmo went on with his story. After an hour, the king ordered him to tell what happened next.

'But that will spoil the story, Kabiyesi, if I tell the end before the middle.'

The king told him to go on with the story and then promptly fell asleep. When he woke up he told everyone to go home.

On the third day the king listened to the story for a while and then sent everyone home again. On the fourth day he asked Tanmo how long it would take the locusts to empty the store.

'I am not sure, Kabiyesi,' Tanmo answered. 'Four thousand and one grains have been taken–about a sack full. There are thousands and thousands of locusts swarming round the store, waiting to go in. Please be patient, Kabiyesi, the locusts are determined.'

'Do you think the store will be empty by the end of the week?'

'The locusts will try their best, Kabiyesi,' answered Tanmo.

The king looked at him and laughed. He turned to his daughter, Enitan, and said, 'This clever young man will surely keep you laughing.'

Enitan had found her husband. She smiled and the crowd cheered.

Tanmo and Enitan had a lovely wedding and lived happily ever after.

13

Asking for too Much

The lion woke up one morning and the first thing he thought about was what to eat for breakfast and lunch and then dinner. He remembered that he had not caught any food the day before. He would have to go hunting and he did not like hunting. He found it boring and annoying.

He got up. I am the king of the jungle, he thought, walking round in circles, his tail flicking from side to side. I shouldn't have to go hunting for food. My food should be brought to me.

The thought of his food beating a path to his door pleased him. He thought about it some more and roared. He was so taken with the idea that he decided to call all the animals in the forest to a meeting. He walked over to the parrot's tree and told her to take a message to all the other animals. He wished to see them about a very important matter. Everyone was to come to his den that evening.

All the animals came at the fixed time and the lion thanked them for coming.

'You have all shown great respect for me as your king and I appreciate this. In the past I have killed some of your friends and relatives as food but I want you to know that it was nothing personal. We all have our different diets. Some of you eat leaves and others eat fruits. This satisfies you. I eat meat and that is why I have called this meeting.'

He told them that it was not right for a king to go hunting for food. Other people would not respect him and if he was not respected, then all the animals would not be respected as well. 'That,' he said, 'is a bad thing.'

To earn the respect of all the people in the world, the lion went on, he wanted all the animals to make a plan for his food to be brought to him. He suggested that they draw up a list. That way everyone would know when it was his or her turn to walk into his den and become his food. There would be no confusion and all the animals would be happy. He would also be happy.

'And we shall have the respect of the whole world,' the lion concluded.

The animals thought about what their king had said. The elephant and the leopard got up and declared that as they were very important animals, almost as important as the lion, they felt it was only right that they should be excused from this plan. The leopard added that to make things easy, the clever fox should draw up the list. He advised that the fox should head the list, to set a good example. All the animals agreed and shouted their approval. The fox drew up a list and put his name first. He told the lion that he would come to be eaten the following morning.

The next day the lion waited for the fox. He waited all day but the fox did not come. The lion became angry. He roared for the parrot and when she came, alarmed, he ordered her to go and call the fox.

The fox turned up some time later.

'I am sorry, Kabiyesi,' he apologised. 'I was on my way here when I met another lion who would not let me pass. He was as big and powerful as you are and there was nothing I could do.

'Another lion? In this forest?' The king was amazed. 'There is no other lion in this forest as big and powerful as me. And if there is, I shall have to get rid of him.'

'I think you should do that, my lord,' said the fox.

'Where is this lion?'

Rosalie · Ann

'Just past the *Odan* tree,' the fox answered 'I'll take you there.'

'Well, what are you waiting for? Lead on,' commanded the lion.

The fox led the lion to a deep well beside the *Odan* tree. He leaned over the edge of the well and pointed inside.

'There!' he announced. 'There is the lion.'

The king looked into the well and saw another lion. He roared and the lion roared back at him. He shook a paw and the lion did the same. The king roared again and then jumped into the well to fight the lion.

The fox and the parrot watched him drown.

'Foolish beast,' the fox said to the parrot, 'asking us to walk to our deaths. Was that how animals walked to meet his forefathers?'

14

The Sea Comes to Visit

A long time ago, when the world was young, before human beings and animals were created, the Sun and the Sea were good friends. The Sun lived on a mountaintop and the Sea lived in a valley. They saw each other every day but it was always the Sun who went down into the valley to visit the Sea.

One day the Sun asked himself why the Sea never came to see him. Does he think I am too poor to host him? Maybe he's not really my friend ... true friends return visits. He thought about it some more and then decided to ask the Sea.

The next time he went into the valley, the Sun asked the Sea why he never came to the mountaintop. 'I come down every day,' he complained, 'and yet you never return my visits.'

The Sea tried to soothe him. He smiled and said that many times he had wished he could visit the Sun. 'We are friends and I like you a lot,' he said. 'I like it when you visit me but if I should visit you, I am afraid you will not, er ... enjoy it.'

'What do you mean?' asked the Sun, even more upset, his face a bright hot orange.

'How do you know if I'll enjoy it or not, if you never come?'

'You don't understand,' said the Sea.

'Oh, I do. It's because you think I am not good enough for you, that's why you won't come.'

There was no convincing the Sun and so the Sea promised to visit him at dawn the next morning.

Rosalie-Ann

The next day the Sun woke up very early. His friend the Sea was visiting and he wanted everything perfect. He got the Wind to clean the mountaintop and also make some music. He stood on his high perch and waited for the Sea.

And the Sea came. He rose up the mountain, flowing into nooks and crannies, climbing plants, swallowing everything in his path. The Sun watched, his mouth open, as the sea covered trees and rocks, and kept coming. He could not believe there was so much of him; the Sea was everywhere. The Sun grew afraid as he watched the mountains disappear into the Sea's wide mouth. He suddenly understood what the Sea had tried to tell him, but it was too late. The Sea kept coming. The Sun jumped onto a higher mountain and the Sea followed him. The Sun hopped from mountaintop to mountaintop until there was nowhere high enough to escape from the Sea. He looked behind him and saw that the world was one great big Sea. Desperate, he turned and fled into the sky, where he lives to this day.

15

The Reward

The war was over but the suffering continued. There was very little food to eat. Most people ate only once a day–small meals that were just enough to keep them alive. Meat was so scarce that no one ate any. It was a difficult time.

One day, after the king had not eaten any meat in several weeks, he announced that he would give a handsome reward to anyone who could bring him some. The news was spread around the town for all to hear.

There were two friends in town who had both fought in the war. One lost his sight and the other both legs. They were a happy pair in spite of their troubles, and they often sat under the trees in the Town Square, talking and laughing. When they heard the king's announcement, they were both excited. They had learnt how to shoot during the war and both of them were quite famous as marksmen.

'We can get the reward,' said the blind man, whose name was Afoju.

'I know,' his friend, Adete, said. 'But don't you think there is a small problem?'

'What problem?' Afoju asked. 'We go into the forest, we look for meat, we shoot it we come back. No problem.'

'How do we hunt and shoot? You can't see and I can't walk.'

'Ah ... I'll tell you.'

Afoju told Adete his plan. He would provide a gun. He would also carry Adete on his back while they hunted for game. Adete would point the way. If they found any game, it was

Adete's job to shoot.

Both friends thought it was a wonderful plan and they set off immediately. Afoju carried Adete into the forest and, following his instructions, continued to carry him as they hunted. After a long time Adete saw an antelope. He told Afoju to crouch without making any noise while he shot at the antelope. He hit the animal but it did not fall. It ran deeper into the bush. The two friends were disappointed and Adete blamed himself. Afoju told him not to worry, that he would carry him further, to look for the animal.

'We can't give up now,' he said, 'and leave the animal for someone else to pick up.' They searched until it was dark and just when they were about to stop and go home, Adete saw the antelope where it had fallen at the edge of the forest. He led Afoju to it, and they picked it up and headed back to town.

They carried the antelope to the palace, eager to see the king. To their surprise, and dismay, when they saw the king he said he could reward only one of them. 'It's one animal you have brought, so, one person gets the reward,' said Kabiyesi.

'Whose animal is it?' he asked.

The two friends were silent.

'I,' Adete started, pointing to his eyes, 'saw the antelope. I shot it dead and I also found the body.'

The people listening nodded.

'I did everything needed to kill the animal,' he continued, 'and, therefore, I believe I should get the reward.'

The crowd cheered its approval.

Afoju agreed that Adete had indeed found the animal. 'I know, my friend, that you can see, but seeing alone does not kill an animal. Whose gun did you use? And how did you get there? Did you fly?'

He turned to the crowd, 'I ask you all, would he have been able to kill the antelope if I had not carried him into the forest? And

after he killed it, who brought him and the animal home? And then to the palace?'

The crowd shouted, 'YOU!'

'Yes,' Afoju nodded. 'If I had not carried him and the animal here, would the king have believed that he killed it? Dear friends, if seeing an animal is the same as killing it, then thinking that one is a king is being a king.'

The crowd clapped at Afoju's eloquence but some felt that Adete's case was just as strong. The counsellors, and even the king, were also not sure. After much thought the king declared that if people worked together, it was only right that they shared the income from their efforts. He divided the reward and gave half to each of the hunters.

16

A World of Wisdom

Everyone knew Tortoise was a wise and clever animal, and no one knew it better than Tortoise himself. Many mornings he would wake up, remember how clever he was, smile contentedly and go back to sleep.

He woke up one morning and a thought came to him. Maybe there was more wisdom in the world than he knew? Maybe, just maybe, there was someone else who knew this and was now gathering all the wisdom? This person would then be wiser and cleverer ... No! Tortoise jumped out of bed and rushed out of the house. I must gather all the wisdom in the world before someone else does, he thought. No one must be wiser than me. He was well on the road into town before he realised that he had nothing to keep the wisdom in, so he went back home and got himself a gourd. It was a brown and black gourd with a narrow, curved neck and a round, wide body.

Tortoise set off on a long journey. He crossed rivers and streams and climbed many hills. As he went along he stopped many times to pick up bits of wisdom, which he stored in his gourd. After he had wandered about for many months he decided that he had collected all the wisdom in the world. He tied a rope around the gourd and hung it around his neck. He was very careful with the gourd; all the wisdom of the world was in it.

He decided to hide the gourd where nobody would ever find it. There was a tall tree in the forest near his village. It was the tallest

Rosalie-Ann

tree in the kingdom and Tortoise decided to hide the gourd at the top of this tree. He headed for the tree, carefully avoiding other animals so that no one would ask him what he was doing. After dodging behind bushes and going down secret paths, he got to the tree. It really was a very tall tree and Tortoise was taken aback at first. How am I going to climb this tree? he wondered.

Since there was no one to answer or help him, he decided to climb it slowly. With the gourd hanging on his chest, he started to climb the tree. He went up a few feet and slid down. He tried again and slid down. He did this several times and every time he fell, he held the gourd up so as not to break it. He fell so many times that he got bruised and battered all over.

Hare was passing by and stopped to watch.

'What are you trying to do?' he asked.

Now, everyone knew Hare was not very clever. Tortoise got up from his last fall, brushed off twigs and soil and told a quick lie.

'There's poison in this gourd. The *babalawo* told me to hide it at the top of the tallest tree. No one must see what is in it ... it's very dangerous.'

Hare nodded. 'If you want to climb the tree you should hang the gourd on your back.'

Tortoise looked at the gourd on his chest and felt foolish. He had been so worried about breaking the gourd that he had not thought of hanging it on his back when he tried to climb the tree. Hare went on his way as Tortoise swung the gourd onto his back and started to climb. He got halfway, easily, and then stopped. He came down slowly. He took the gourd off his neck and smashed it against a rock.

'If stupid Hare is wise enough to show me how to climb, then I can't have all the wisdom in the world,' he said angrily. 'No one can have it all.'

17

The Honey Guide

Koko the farmer was lost in the forest. He had overheard a story about an amazing palm tree in the forest and had come searching for it. The tree had the best palm-oil nuts Koko had ever heard about and he had decided to find the tree and collect as many nuts as he could. He did not let anyone know when he left the village because he wanted to keep all the nuts for himself.

Now he was lost. No one would look for him because no one knew he was missing. They would think he was on his farm. He wandered around in the forest for three days until he came to a large *Iroko* tree. He was hungry and tired so he sat down to rest for a while. Just as he was about to continue searching for a way out of the forest, he heard a bird calling from above him. He looked up and saw a small purple and blue bird.

'Who are you?' he asked.

'I am the honey guide,' the bird answered, alighting on a branch near him.

Koko had heard about the honey guide. The bird knew all the honeybee hives in the forest and often led hunters to them. Koko's mouth watered and his stomach rumbled.

'My good friend,' he said, 'I have a little problem and I wonder if you can help me.'

The honey guide replied that she was always ready to help. 'What is your problem?' she asked.

'I am a bit lost,' Koko said, 'and I have not eaten for two days. Can you help me?'

'Oh, I can,' the bird answered. 'If you follow me, I'll lead you to some sweet honey ... and then to the river.'

'That's ... that's wonderful! I can find my way from the river.'

The honey guide flew in front of Koko. She would fly a short distance and then wait for him to catch up. She did this until they got to a hive. The bird sat quietly on a branch and watched as Koko reached into the hive and brought out the honeycomb. He ate all of the honey quickly, licking his lips and swallowing greedily.

When he had finished, he turned to the bird and asked for more. 'That was nice!' he declared. 'Let's look for some more.'

'I see you have eaten it all,' the bird sighed.

Koko felt guilty. 'It wasn't very much,' he said, 'and you know I haven't eaten in a long, long time.'

The bird did not answer.

'I'll leave some for you next time,' he continued. 'I promise I will.'

The bird led him to another hive. Again Koko ate greedily without leaving anything for his guide and again he promised to leave some the next time. 'I forgot,' he pleaded, doing his best to look sorry.

He did the same thing a third time. 'I forgot,' he repeated and promised that he would not forget the next time.

The bird did not say anything. She led him on and when she got near another hive, she told him that he would have to climb to reach it. She perched on a nearby tree and waited. The hive was high up in the tree and Koko climbed eagerly to reach it. As he poked into the hive, a swarm of bees poured out and before he could say or do anything they were all over him buzzing and stinging. He scrambled down the tree, shouting for help.

'Bees! Bees!' he screamed. 'Why didn't you tell me?'

'I forgot,' the honey guide said mildly, and watched as Koko jumped up and raced into the forest, slapping himself all over as he ran. The bees followed, a thick, angry cloud that stung him again and again. The bird watched them go and then flew to the hive where she ate the honey and the little grubs that Koko had brought out and dropped.

18

The Rich Man and the Poor Man

Many rains ago, in a village on the plains, there lived two friends. One was rich and the other was poor, but they lived near each other happily. The poor man worked for the rich man, looking after his crops and tending his cattle.

Now, it happened that there was a drought. The crops withered and died, and the cattle grew so thin you could hear their bones clacking when they walked. Everyone was hungry. The poor man went to beg the rich man for food. He took his poor wife and his poor children along.

The rich man became angry. 'This is the problem with poor people!' he shouted. 'They are always there when you don't need them.' He chased the poor man away.

One day, a farmer saw the poor man looking for food and pitied him. He gave him some maize. The poor man took the maize back to his hut and showed his wife. She cooked it but as they did not have meat to make a stew, or even salt to make the meal tasty, it was a very poor fare.

The poor man said, 'I'll go and see my rich friend.'

When he got to the rich man's house he found the gate locked. He knocked but no one answered. As he stood by the gate, an appetising aroma that made his knees shake drifted from the house. He went back to his hut, took the maize-meal and returned to the rich man's house. He sat by the wall and ate his food while breathing in the aroma of the rich man's dinner.

A few days later he met the rich man and told him about it. 'And I really enjoyed my meal,' he said. 'The delicious smell of

Rosalie-Ann

your food made it the best meal I've had in weeks.'

The rich man was furious. 'So that is why my food was tasteless that day!' he screamed 'You stole the sweet smell! You must pay for it!'

He was so angry that he went straight to the judge and reported the case. He asked for a goat as payment. The poor man was called before the judge and he was told to pay for the sweet smell of the rich man's food.

'We can't have this kind of nonsense in my town!' the judge thundered. 'You are to pay him one goat! I'll give you till tomorrow.'

The poor man was stunned. 'A goat? A whole goat?' he whispered.

He did not know what to do. On his way home he met a friend, the village Imam. He told him the story and his friend told him not to worry.

The next day the poor man went to the Imam's house. The Imam gave him a goat and went with him to the court. A crowd had gathered to watch.

'Where is the goat?' the judge asked.

'It is here, your honour,' the Imam said, 'but I have one or two things to say.'

The judge nodded.

'If my friend had eaten the rich man's food, then, indeed, he must give back the food,' the Imam stated, 'but since it was the smell he breathed, along with everyone else who passed by, it is my opinion that it is the smell he must return.'

'But how can he pay back the smell of the food?' the crowd asked.

'I will show you.' He dragged the goat forward. 'You have demanded a goat,' he said to the rich man. 'Here is the goat.'

The rich man got up eagerly.

'But,' the Imam halted him with a raised forefinger, 'you can only take the smell. The poor man did not take your food; he breathed the smell. So, you cannot take the goat ... but you can have it's smell.'

The crowd cheered and clapped loudly. They liked the decision. The rich man was speechless.

19

Gizo the Spider

This tale about Gizo happened a long time ago. This was a time when the world was still new and the gods often spoke to people and animals.

Gizo lived in a small village and of all the animals and people in the village, Gizo was the laziest and trickiest. Now, spiders are not known for hard work; they spin their webs and lie in wait. But even amongst spiders Gizo was an exception. He did not toil, neither did he spin. Yet he always got everything he wanted.

One day Gizo needed a gift for his mother-in-law. It was the custom to send gifts at harvest time but since Gizo did not sow, he had nothing to reap. He set out from home jauntily, singing and swinging his machete in time with his song. He had not the slightest doubt that he would find a gift. On his way he came to an oil-palm plantation. The kernels on the trees were ripe and hung in big red bunches. Ah, said Gizo to himself, this is it!

He swarmed up the trees, one after the other, as if he was possessed. For someone so lazy, he worked really quickly and in a short time he had cut several bunches. Gizo knew that the thief who is slow is the thief who is caught. He gathered the kernels and got out his bag. As he was filling his bag he heard a noise. Someone was coming. From the loud confident way the person moved through the plantation, Gizo knew it had to be the owner. He dropped everything and ran. The farmer heard him, came upon the bag of kernels and the machete, and chased after the raider. Gizo was nowhere to be seen; he had gone where the smoke from the cooking fire goes.

The farmer took away the bag and the machete. He wanted to see the person who would claim them. Gizo did not try to claim his things. The thought did not even occur to him. What he did was to sit and think of a trick to get back the bag of kernels and his machete from the farmer.

At that time everybody believed that God lived on top of the highest mountain in the world. Whenever God had something to say, God came down and sat on the tallest tree in the neighbourhood. No one dared to look on God's face and none questioned God's demands. God was the Giver-of-all-things and the Bringer-of-rain. God's word was law. Gizo knew all these things. Close to his village was a mighty Iroko tree from the top of which God spoke to the villagers. Early one morning, before anyone woke up, Gizo decided to play God. He climbed to the top of the Iroko tree and hid there. A little while later he saw the farmer on his way to his farm. Gizo waited until the farmer was passing beneath the Iroko tree and then, in a deep voice that he thought must be like God's, he started to sing:

Give the machete to God
Kia-kia
And the bag of kernels
Kia-kia
Add some yam and maize
Kia-kia
It is God who commands
Kia-kia

When the farmer heard the song he was afraid. God must be keeping a close watch on him. He ran back to his house, got the machete and the bag of kernels and some yam and maize from his store, and took them all to the Iroko tree. He crept towards the tree; his eyes fixed on the ground. He did not look up and he did not speak. This was the proper behaviour in God's presence. The farmer dropped his load and

Rosalie-Ann

then crept back to his house. He gathered his family inside and locked the door firmly. No one was going out until they felt the Giver-of-all-things had had enough time to receive the offering.

Gizo the spider patted himself on the back with all eight hands (or feet). He carried everything away. The farmer came out later and saw that his offering had been accepted. He stood up straight and smiled broadly. 'God is on my side,' he said.

20

Day and Night

A long time ago, when men and animals spoke the same language and God spoke to all, some villagers complained that they did not like the night. 'The day's alright,' they said, 'but the night, and the dark ...' They shook their heads.

'We are afraid of the dark.'

'We cannot see.'

'We cannot look after our cattle.'

The animals felt the same way and so a meeting was called to decide what to do. The elders spoke first. One said, 'We should light huge fires all night long.'

Another said, 'Everyone should carry a little lamp at night.'

Then one of the oldest and wisest men spoke. He was a medicine man and everyone kept quiet while he spoke. 'We must ask God to give us two suns,' he said slowly and weightily. 'One sun will rise in the east and the other will rise in the west. That way there will never be darkness again.'

All the people and the animals shouted in agreement.

Then a small voice said, 'But ... but how will we get any shade?'

The medicine man bristled. 'Who said that,' he shouted.

No one answered. The animal with the small voice was too afraid to speak up. But one of the men in the crowd, a tall strong warrior, had seen the little animal.

'It was the hare who spoke,' the warrior said.

The hare tried to hide in the crowd but he was fished out and placed in the middle where the great wise elders sat.

Rosalie-Ann

The old medicine man glared at him. 'How dare you disagree with your elders?' he said. 'What do you know about such matters?'

'I, I don't know anything,' the little hare quivered.

'Speak up, hare,' the medicine-man sneered, 'we await your wisdom.'

All the people and animals laughed–all but the warrior who had first seen the hare.

'Don't be afraid of them,' he said. 'Speak.' He prodded the hare with his spear to get him going.

The hare looked up at him and felt braver.

'All I wanted to say was that if we had two suns, there wouldn't be any shade. We won't be able to sleep and the cattle will die of heat and thirst. The waters of the lakes and rivers and streams will dry up. The trees will die. Then there will be hunger in the land, and we shall all die.'

There was silence when the hare finished speaking.

After a while the old medicine man got up. 'Indeed you are the wisest of us all, little hare,' he said.

Everyone agreed and they accepted the wise words of the little hare. And till this day they have both day and night.